D0119365

Hieroglyph
Edition

TRANSLATORS' NOTE

The Tale of Peter Rabbit has already been translated into thirty-five languages, including Latin and Lowland Scots. The time seemed appropriate to attempt a translation into the hieroglyphic script of ancient Egypt, but three major problems presented themselves. First, all knowledge of the ancient Egyptian language was lost between the fifth century AD and the work of Åkerblad, Thomas Young and, particularly, Champollion in 1822. Secondly, the environment, flora and fauna of England in the time of Beatrix Potter all differed radically from those of Egypt four thousand years ago. Thirdly, the literary traditions and styles of England and Egypt are very different.

Our understanding of the ancient Egyptian language remains limited by the resources available to us. These include monumental inscriptions and a wide range of papyri, mostly written in the cursive hieratic script, which include letters, also written in hieratic. Our knowledge of the spoken language is limited to quotations of direct speech in certain papyri and occasional comments inscribed above depictions of workers in tomb paintings. We can only guess at pronunciation. Limited help is available from the Coptic language, which developed from ancient Egyptian in the second century AD and is still spoken in church ceremonies today.

The Egyptians themselves regarded the classical phase of the ancient Egyptian language as that of the Middle Kingdom, c. 2055–1795 BC. We have opted for the grammatical style and vocabulary of this period, during which many classical literary works were written, including *The Tale of the Court of King Cheops* (on the Westcar Papyrus, P. Berlin 3033) and *The Tale of the Shipwrecked Sailor* (P. Leningrad 1115), which have served as models for our translations. Nevertheless, Beatrix Potter's words sometimes do not readily fall into ancient Egyptian; the surviving texts provide no easy model for such colloquial phrases as 'Now run along, and don't get into mischief'.

Differences between Edwardian England and Pharaonic Egypt provide interesting problems in vocabulary. Most fundamental is the word for rabbit. Peter was a common European rabbit (*Lepus cuniculus*), which was unknown in Egypt. The only related species was the desert hare (*Lepus capensis*) for which, fortunately, the Egyptian word (*skhat*) is well attested, and this appears early in line 1 of page 7, terminated by the unmistakable determinative of the desert hare. However, it must be stressed that the same hieroglyph is widely used as the biliteral phonetic 'wn' and is, in fact, the first hieroglyph to appear on page 7. The word so formed has nothing to do with *Lepus capensis*.

Another interesting problem was gender discrimination of the desert hare. The names of male and female persons were distinguished in ancient Egyptian by the seated-man or seated-woman determinatives, respectively. No such system existed for distinguishing the sex of animals and, to complicate matters further, the word for desert hare (*skhat*) ends in 't', which is the normal termination for feminine Egyptian words. However, the presentation of Peter's family is so blatantly anthropomorphic that we elected to use the seated-man and seated-woman determinatives after the names of Peter and his sisters.

The wheel was a relatively recent introduction in the ancient Egypt of the Middle Kingdom and, so far as we are aware, was only used on chariots. There is no evidence of the existence of wheelbarrows. So we resorted to the well-known word for sledge. Many botanical species familiar to Peter were quite unknown in ancient Egypt. These include blackberry, gooseberry, black-currant and potato. Footnotes explain how these and other problems were circumvented, in order to convey the sense of this tale in a literary style from a far earlier phase of world literature.

THE TALE OF
Peter Rabbit

The Tale of Peter Rabbit

Beatrix Potter

Hieroglyph Edition

Translated by J.F. Nunn
and R.B. Parkinson

THE BRITISH MUSEUM PRESS

Text © 2005 The Trustees of the British Museum

Hieroglyph edition first published in 2005
by The British Museum Press
A division of The British Museum Company Ltd
38 Russell Square, London WC1B 3QQ

The Tale of Peter Rabbit
First published in Great Britain
by Frederick Warne & Co. Ltd 1902
New reproductions copyright
© Frederick Warne & Co. 2002
Original copyright in text and illustrations
© Frederick Warne & Co. 1902
Frederick Warne & Co. is the owner of all rights, copyrights and trademarks
in the Beatrix Potter character names and illustrations.
www.peterrabbit.com

A catalogue record for this book
is available from the British Library
ISBN-13: 978-0-7141-1969-4

ISBN-10: 0-7141-1969-5

Designed and typeset in ITC Caslon and RabbitType
by John Hawkins Book Design
Hieroglyphs typeset by Nigel Strudwick using
the Cleo Font designed by Cleo Huggins
This edition produced exclusively for
The British Museum Press by Frederick Warne & Co.
Colour reproduction by
EAE Creative Colour Ltd, Norwich
Printed and bound in Italy

PUBLISHER'S NOTE

The full and complete text of this first tale in Beatrix Potter's famous series of little books has here been faithfully translated and transcribed, page for page, into hieroglyphic script, based on the centenary edition published in 2002 by Frederick Warne & Co.

The Translators
John F. Nunn retired as head of the anaesthesia division of the Clinical Research Centre, British Medical Research Council. He is the author of *Ancient Egyptian Medicine* as well as a number of medical monographs and textbooks which have become standard works. He is a member of the Egypt Exploration Society and has been studying Egyptian hieroglyphs for over twenty-five years.

Richard B. Parkinson is an Assistant Keeper in the Department of Ancient Egypt and Sudan in the British Museum. He is an international authority on Ancient Egyptian literature, and his books include *The Tale of Sinuhe and Other Ancient Egyptian Poems*, *Poetry and Culture in Middle Kingdom Egypt* and *Pocket Guide to Ancient Egyptian Hieroglyphs*.

Line 3: 'Cotton-tail' has been translated as 'Linen-tail'  (*sed-mehew*), since cotton was unknown in ancient Egypt.

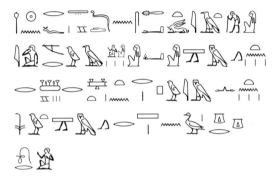

Lines 4–5: Mr. McGregor is written as 'son of Gregor'
(*sa Gregor*).

Line 3: Pies were unknown in ancient Egypt, so pie is written as 'warm bread'  (*te seref*).

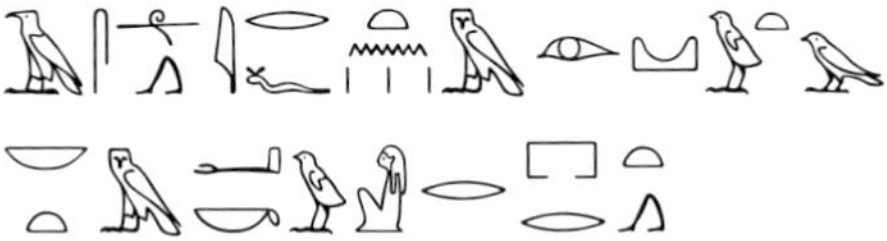

Line 2: The ancient Egyptians had no need for umbrellas, so the word for 'sunshade' 𓇋𓆄𓏭𓏏𓇳 (*shwyt*) has been used.

Line 4: Blackberries were unknown in ancient Egypt and have been replaced here with 'sweet fruit' (*benriwt*), which commonly refers to dates.

Lines 2–3: Charpentier (1981) cites the last two words, (*matt khast*), as 'céleri du désert' (*Apium petroselinum*), or parsley.

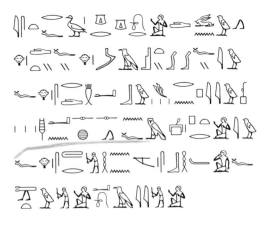

Line 3: There is no doubt about the word for lettuce (probably *Lactuca sativa*) in ancient Egyptian, but we do not know whether they grew cabbages, a species closely related to lettuce. We have therefore used the Egyptian word for 'lettuce' (*abw*).

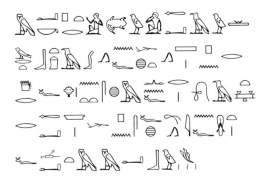

Line 4: The word for 'sandal' (*tchebwt*) has been used for shoe.

It is highly unlikely that the potato was known in
ancient Egypt, so 'apples of the earth'
(*depehew-ta*) has been substituted.

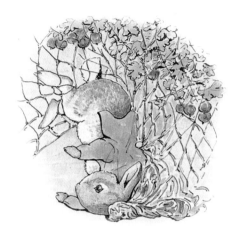

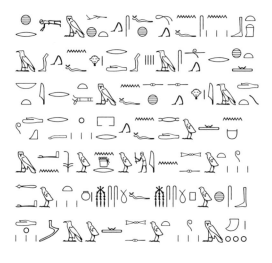

Line 4: Gooseberries were unknown in Egypt and are here translated simply as 'fruit' (*dekerew*).

Lines 3–4: The house sparrow (*Passer domesticus*) was not named in ancient Egypt, but *Passer domesticus aegypticus* appears to be Gardiner's hieroglyph G 37. We have therefore used these hieroglyphs 𓆓𓏤𓅪 (*nedjesw*) to indicate sparrows: 𓆓𓏤𓅪 (*nedjes*) means 'small'.

Line 2: There is no evidence that the ancient Egyptians had anything corresponding to the modern watering can. We have used the word 'jar'  (*des*).

Lines 6–7: Peter's sneeze ('Kertyschoo!') has been rendered phonetically: ⸰⸰⸰ .

43

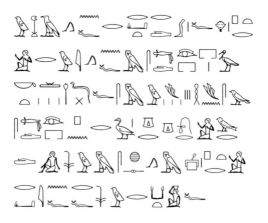

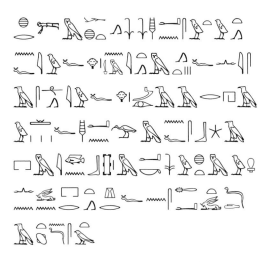

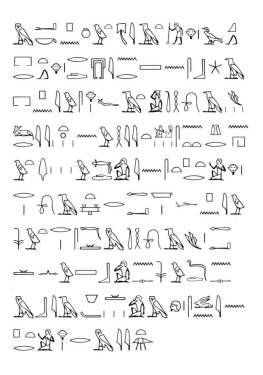

Lines 3–4: For the onomatopoeic 'scr-r-ritch, scratch' (the noise of a hoe), we have used the Egyptian word for hoeing with a sign change to represent 'scritch':

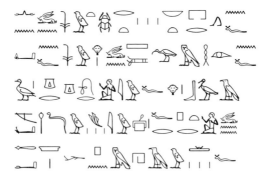

Line 2: Wheels were only used for chariots in the Middle Kingdom of ancient Egypt; wheelbarrow has been translated as 'sledge' (*wenesh*).

Lines 3–4: Black-currant bushes were unknown in ancient Egypt, so they have been translated as 'bushes of black fruit' (*bawt net dekherew kemet*).

Line 2: The word for 'scarecrow' in ancient Egyptian is
unknown. However, the text explains why Mr. McGregor
hung up Peter's jacket and shoes.

60

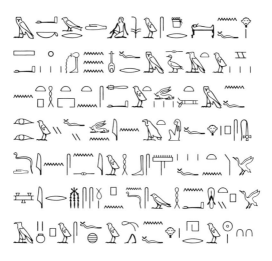

Line 7: The Egyptian week lasted ten days. 'Fortnight' is therefore written as 'twenty days' (*herew 20*).

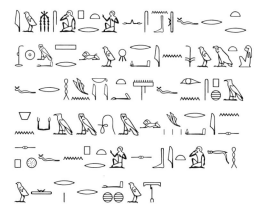

Line 4: Although some variety of camomile probably existed in ancient Egypt, the Egyptian word for the plant remains unknown. The word has therefore simply been transliterated, as for a foreign word:

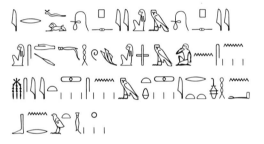

68

For 'The End', we have given the usual Egyptian scribe's colophon, which indicates completion of the manuscript, and may be translated as: 'So it ends, from start to finish as found in the writing of the writer Beatrix Potter'.